The Child's World®

Published in the United States of America by The Child's World®
1980 Lookout Drive • Mankato, MN 56003-1705
800-599-READ • www.childsworld.com

ACKNOWLEDGMENTS
The Child's World®: Mary Berendes, Publishing Director
The Design Lab: Kathleen Petelinsek, Design and Page Production
Literacy Consultants: Cecilia Minden, PhD, and Joanne Meier, PhD

LIBRARY OF CONGRESS
CATALOGING-IN-PUBLICATION DATA
Moncure, Jane Belk.
  My "s" sound box / by Jane Belk Moncure ;
illustrated by Rebecca Thornburgh.
    p. cm. — (Sound box books)
  Summary: "Little s has an adventure with items beginning with
his letter's sound, such as seashells, seven seals, and a sailor who
sails on a submarine."—Provided by publisher.
  ISBN 978-1-60253-159-8 (library bound : alk. paper)
  [1. Alphabet.] I. Thornburgh, Rebecca McKillip, ill. II. Title. III.
Series.
  PZ7.M739Mys 2009
  [E]–dc22   2008033175

A NOTE TO PARENTS AND EDUCATORS:

Magic moon machines and five fat frogs are just a few of the fun things you can share with children by reading books with them. Reading aloud helps children in so many ways! It introduces them to new words, motivates them to develop their own reading skills, and expands their attention span and listening abilities. So it's important to find time each day to share a book or two . . . or three!

As you read with young children, you can help develop their understanding of how print works by talking about the parts of the book—the cover, the title, the illustrations, and the words that tell the story. As you read, use your finger to point to each word, modeling a gentle sweep from left to right.

Simple word games help develop important prereading skills, including an understanding of rhyme and alliteration (when words share the same beginning sound, such as "six" and "sand"). Try playing with words from a book you've just shared: "What other words start with the same sound as moon?" "Cat and hat, do those words rhyme?" The possibilities are endless—and so are the rewards!

My "s" Sound Box®

(The "sh" sound is included in this book along with blends.)

WRITTEN BY JANE BELK MONCURE

ILLUSTRATED BY REBECCA THORNBURGH

Little had a box. "I will find things that begin with my **S** sound," he said. "I will put them into my sound box."

Little  took off his shoes, socks, sweater, and shirt. Did he put his shoes, socks, sweater, and shirt into his box? He did.

Little  put on his swimsuit and his sandals. He went for a walk on the sand.

He found a shovel and a sand pail.

He made a sand castle. Then he

put the shovel, the sand pail, and

the sand castle into his box.

Little 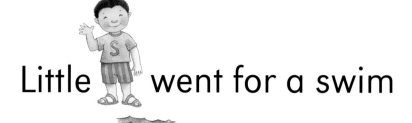 went for a swim

in the sea.

He saw a seal swimming in  the sea.

He saw six more seals on the

sand. Did he put the seven seals

into his box? He did.

Little  found seashells all over the sand.

He also found a starfish. Did
he put the seashells and the
starfish into his box? He did.

Then he saw a shark. It was a small shark. So Little  slipped it into a sack. He put the sack into the box.

Then Little  saw a sea snake.

It was a small sea snake. So he

slipped the snake into the sack.

He put the sack back into the box.

Later, Little  met a sailor.

The  sailor gave him a sailor hat.

"Let's play!" said the  sailor.

They played on the seesaw.

They slid down the slide.

They swung on the swings.

Suddenly, there was a big noisy

sound! The sound was coming

from the box.

"What is in the box?" asked

the  sailor.

"Things that begin with my S sound," said Little  .

"I sail on things that begin with

your **S** sound," said the  sailor.

"I sail on a ship."

"And I sail on a submarine."

The  sailor helped Little  bring his box into the submarine. Little  took his things out of his box.

Little  and the sailor drew pictures of the ship, the swing, the slide, and the seesaw.

Little 's Word List

sack	seal 	shovel
sailor 	seashell	slide
sailor hat	sea snake	sock
sand	seesaw	starfish
sandal	shark 	submarine
sand castle	ship	sweater
sand pail 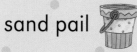	shirt	swimsuit
sea	shoe	swing

Other Words with Little

salad

snow

squirrel

sandwich

soap

stamp

saw

soup

star

seed

spider

stick

skunk

spoon

stop sign

snail

square

sun

More to Do!

Little  and the sailor talked about lots of different **S** words. They put many **S** things into the box. You can make cards of all the **S** things.

What you need:

- index cards
- crayons
- markers
- yarn
- hole punch tool

Directions:

1. Draw a picture of these **S** words on the index cards:

- sack
- sand pail
- seal
- sea snake
- shark

- ship
- shoe
- sock
- starfish
- swing

2. After you have your picture cards, have an adult help you sort the pictures into two piles: sea creatures and not-sea creatures.

3. Put all the cards together again. Now sort the cards into two new piles: things you play with and things you don't play with.

4. Put all the cards together again. Now try writing each word below the picture you drew. Have an adult help you write down the sounds you hear in each word.

5. Now use the hole-punching tool to make a hole in the corner of each card. Pull some yarn through and make your very own **S** book!

About the Author

Best-selling author Jane Belk Moncure has written over 300 books throughout her teaching and writing career. After earning a Master's degree in Early Childhood Education from Columbia University, she became one of the pioneers in that field. In 1956, she helped form the Virginia Association for Early Childhood Education, which established the first statewide standards for teachers of young children.

Inspired by her work in the classroom, Mrs. Moncure's books have become standards in primary education, and her name is recognized across the country. Her success is reflected not only in her books' popularity with parents, children, and educators, but also by numerous awards, including the 1984 C. S. Lewis Gold Medal Award.

About the Illustrator

Rebecca Thornburgh lives in a pleasantly spooky old house in Philadelphia. If she's not at her drawing table, she's reading—or singing with her band, called Reckless Amateurs. Rebecca has one husband, two daughters, and two silly dogs.